The Secrets of 24 Blackwe

Description:

The stories and other snippets herein ar
the attractive and historic little building, ᴋ..ᴜwıı as number 24,
Blackwellgate, Darlington.

They tend towards the supernatural including time travel, witchcraft and other spooky stuff.

They also touch upon social issues of the times they are set in, such as attitudes towards family values, same-sex love, relationships, religion, the class system and so on…

This volume completes a series of two books, which cover various periods in time up to and including the present.

The Secrets of 24 Blackwellgate - Book Two

"Many thanks must go to Tony and Colin for putting up with me when I was working on this book and to Dave Shaw for taking the photograph of us all on the stairs of 24, Blackwellgate"
~Beryl.

The Secrets of 24 Blackwellgate - Book Two

Acknowledgements

Front cover image by Paul Magrs
Design elements by Jake Todhunter

Photographs or images used which are not our own, are credited separately

Book one and book two are both available to buy in store or online, from Guru Boutique, 24 Blackwellgate, Darlington, DL1 5HG or www.guruboutique.co.uk

Tel:01325461479

Other suppliers are Lulu.com, Amazon and the usual online sites plus most good bookshops.

Price £5.99

Published by Lulu.com for Guru Publications

Copyright belongs to Beryl Hankin
© 2018 and onwards infinitum

More acknowledgements

Special mention must go to the lady who gave Guru Boutique many of the objects, which inspired three of my own stories in this book series. I just wish I had taken her name and details so that I could thank her properly.
I really must try and find her again, as at the time I had no idea that her kind gifts would lead to a trilogy of stories.

I must also give a nod to the following lovely people....

Bridget Lowery and Rachal 'Moonflower' Davidson) for their stories in book one of this series. I very much regret that various other demands on their time prevented all three of us collaborating on this second book also

Courtney Stanley, for being the embodiment of my character Sarah as a young girl.

Michelle Sambora, for the great detective work.

Kailee-Ray Horner and Heather Horner, for travelling to Darlington with their family albums.
Lennon, for being the gorgeous little boy that he is.
Barbara Horner, for being my beautiful Auntie Barbara.

Kirk and Julie Donnelly, for being the guardians of Nana Tanner's impressive photograph collection.

Mervena Conroy, for all her enthusiasm and for being such a fabulous cousin.

Last, but certainly not least, all the people who are interested in reading these stories, for supporting our scribbles.

Dedication

"I dedicate this book to number 24, Blackwellgate, Darlington for the inspiration and pleasure it has provided and continues to provide, to myself, and many others, over the years" ~Beryl.

The Secrets of 24 Blackwellgate - Book Two

Number 24 Blackwellgate, Darlington

The Secrets of 24 Blackwellgate - Book Two

Contents:

THICKER THAN WATER

FAMILY ALBUM

THE OBJECTS OF 24, BLACKWELLGATE

1. The Monkey Skull
2. Daisy Dunne's Tiny Tea Pot
3. Band Of Gold
4. Padfoot And The Ten Bob Note
5. Joan Of Wad & Jack'O'Lantern
6. Sarah Susannah's Lamp

TRICK OR TREAT?
.

(Author: Beryl Maughan Hankin)

P.S. "There are bound to be more and even deeper secrets connected to this magical building. One day all may be revealed…" ~ Beryl

The Secrets of 24 Blackwellgate - Book Two

The basement in number 24, Blackwellgate, which in itself is an inspiration. - (Photo by Irene Ross)

The story, which follows, is the last in a trilogy and although it can be read as a stand alone, it may help the reader to understand some aspects of it better if I include the following introduction....

PROLOGUE

My name is Beryl Hankin.
I live in the here and now and although I know this may sound strange,
I have a friend from the past.

I work as a shopkeeper in an old building, which bears the address of 24, Blackwellgate, Darlington.
It is the same address and location that a young woman named Sarah Susannah Wheeler and her family lived, worked and had adventures in during the 1800's. By some quirk of fate and for reasons, which we never fully understood (apart from suspecting it all involved parallel universe's converging at a particular physical spot), Sarah and I discovered that we could meet across time.
Once we had recovered from the initial shock, we became firm friends and both of us realised how lucky we were to be able to do this.
Sarah was first a loving daughter, then a ladies maid/companion and subsequently (partly due to our meetings and conversations), a popular writer of science fiction.
We even managed to sustain our unusual friendship when she moved to London to be nearer to her publisher and to lodge with her brother and a dear friend, because we still had the basement of number 24 as our secret meeting place.

On my part I delighted in finding out, through talking to Sarah, what it was like to live in this town we were both born into, back in her day. She on the other hand was always amazed at my accounts of how much the world had changed from what was considered to be normal back then. She had even been able to use the information she got from our conversations in her stories, and also to re-assure her beloved brother Simon and his male lover Jimmy Nicholson that one day loving relationships such as theirs would be openly celebrated and totally legal. She confided to me that they didn't quite believe her when, after our conversations, she would return to London, brimming with what they considered to be wild ideas. I can recall her giggling and telling me that they just thought it was the writer in her talking. They couldn't really see the things she described ever happening, but she knew her words gave them comfort.

It was not just the thrill of sharing knowledge that had brought us so close, however. It was the fact that we felt connected in some other very deep sort of way, which neither of us understood.

It was vital that our meetings took place under this particular roof, as it was the only place we knew of where our two lives could converge and where we had established a point of contact ever since.

Given the fact that by now in Sarah's time zone, she had left Darlington and her mother had moved to a grand house called Chorley Hall to become companion to Mrs Nicholson (Sarah's ex employer), you may be wondering how we were still able to use this location?

Well, we'd talked about it and made a plan.

Sarah got Simon (who used to have his photographic studio at 24 Blackwellgate), to make an arrangement with the tenant of the property, Mrs Thorpe, to sub-rent part of the basement as a storage area for the surplus equipment he had left behind when he moved to London. Sarah also made sure she also had the right of entrance as well. This worked really well for us as we could both be alone down there on many occasions and enjoy each other's company in privacy. From my end it was an excellent arrangement, of course, as here in the present I worked in this building almost every day.

Then suddenly Sarah's visits ceased.

At first I was waiting for her to come back but as the months went by I realised this may not happen and that made me very sad.

I moped about wondering what had happened to her and her family to prevent her from seeing me. It seemed cruel that we had been allowed to become so close only to have this special relationship taken away. I worried that something bad had occurred, as I knew that if she possibly could she would cross that time barrier to be here with me whenever she was back in our town.

It's very scary to love a building so much that it sometimes seems to be an extension of one's own self or even that one's self is an extension of it. I have always known, of course, that number 24 Blackwellgate was the perfect home for our business, but I also knew there was even more to it than that and somehow it was connected to both Sarah and myself.

The very idea of ever vacating these premises before I knew the full significance of it all, terrified me in the extreme. Eventually I resorted to desperate measures in an effort to discover some answers. I needed to know why I was so attached to this place and why within these walls, I alone had managed bridge the gap between present and past and form a real bond with a girl from another era?

Thankfully, I did eventually discover the answer I needed. It is shared, for anyone who is curious, within the pages of the following story…

THICKER THAN WATER (by Beryl Maughan Hankin)

PART ONE

The year was 1878 and it was a Sunday afternoon in Jimmy Nicholson's London apartment.
Simon and Sarah Wheeler were teasing each other noisily as brothers and sisters do, whilst Jimmy laughingly protested that he was trying to read a book.

These three were happy and content in each other's company.
They cared for one another, they enjoyed their London lives and their situation was as secure as anyone's can be.
Jimmy was wealthy anyway and the other two had employment, which brought in enough respective amounts of money to allow them to be free of financial worry. Life was good.
The only secret between them was the fact that Sarah never revealed to them her ability to move between time zones.
It was several weeks since Sarah had returned from one of her trips back to her hometown of Darlington, to visit her own mother (Barbara Wheeler) and Jimmy's mother (Eleanor Nicholson) who was her former employer, mentor and friend.
She had also made her regular journey in order to see a secret friend from the future, but the others were not aware of this.

Reluctantly, due to the increasing hilarity of his two companions, Jimmy finally admitted defeat and laid down the book they were preventing him from concentrating on.
His eyes alighted on a pile of mail which had arrived over the last few days, but which he had delayed from opening. Amongst it was an envelope addressed to Mr Simon and Miss Sarah S Wheeler. He recognised their mother's handwriting on it so he passed it over to Simon to open.
The news was not happy. Barbara Wheeler's words told of the sad death of their friend Mrs Thorpe who was the tenant of number 24 Blackwellgate, which at one time had been the Wheeler's family home too. The letter went on to say that the premises had been sold and the new occupiers were intent on turning it from commercial premises, back into a family home, so had requested that all the items stored there which belonged to Simon Wheeler should be removed as soon as possible. The locks would be changed and right to access terminated.
Barbara Wheeler went on to say that as the agreement to occupy the basement had been an informal one, she had taken it upon herself

(with Eleanor Nicholson's permission) to have all the contents of the basement which belonged to her son brought to Chorley Hall for safe keeping, until such time as Simon could return to sort it out.
This news came as a great shock to the young people hearing it, as 24 Blackwellgate had special meaning for them all. Sarah, however, was the most affected, because she realised that not being able to access the location would prevent her from seeing her friend from the future.
She began to sob as she realised they would probably not even be able to say goodbye. Simon and Jimmy tried to comfort her but were a little puzzled as to why this development was affecting her so much. After all, sad as it was, Mrs Thorpe's death had been that of a family friend rather than someone with closer ties to them all.

PART TWO

I hadn't had any contact with Sarah Wheeler, my dear friend from the past, for well over a year now but Sarah was always in my mind. How could she not be, as our relationship had been so extra-ordinary?
Eventually I could bear the silence no longer and decided to try and do something about it.
It was a really long shot, but Sarah had told me that she, Simon and Jimmy had a favourite place in London where they used to go on a regular basis. It was a public house frequented by artists, writers and the like, called The Artichoke, so I decided to focus my efforts on trying to resume contact there. I did some research and found that there had been a place of that name in Kensington, which was in the area I knew Jimmy's apartment was situated in. I also learnt that there was still a pub operating on the same spot that The Artichoke had occupied, so that had to be the one. To my pleasant surprise, a bit more research informed me that The Artichoke was now called The Prince of Wales, in Kensington Church Street, which, as it turned out

was a favourite place of mine too. This was great news and allowed me to hope that my long shot was now looking a bit more promising. I could remember the establishment well from the visits I had made there with my late mother, Irene and Tony and Colin, the guys from our shop.
The reason we had been drawn to that pub on so many happy occasions seemed to make a lot more sense to me now.
I could picture it in my mind's eye. It was a traditional London pub with a bow window and a narrow entrance from the street. A long bar ran along one side and you could not only get a drink there but also, if you were hungry, sit in and eat some lunch (which was always steak and ale pie in our case). There were some nice old wooden booths containing tables for this purpose. They had a great jukebox too and we always started off our selection with Baker Street by Gerry Rafferty. Those are happy, happy, memories. In addition to the things I just described, the feature I was drawn to the most in this great little hostelry was the huge mirror that formed the whole of the back wall. It was edged with a gilt frame, which fit exactly into the space it occupied. The glass was yellowed and cloudy and pleasingly mottled with age.
I always wondered just how many cigars and pipes must have been enjoyed in there over the years to cause this unique effect.
I loved that mirror and felt as if I could be happy to stand in front of it forever, just gazing into it and imagining all the other eyes in the other faces, which had done the same before me.

Now I was intending to visit there again, in the hope that my Sarah might be gazing into the same mirror at the same moment as I, but in another time. Surely if we could synchronize in this way, we would be re-united? It was a slender hope but the only one I had.

I really couldn't afford either the time off work or the fare to London on the train, but this was something I had to do regardless.

My friends and family thought I was mad to take off like this, especially on the run up to Christmas when there was so much work to be done at the shop, but I just told them I needed some time to myself and went anyway.
Once off the train I didn't even check into my hotel, but took a taxi straight to Kensington Church Street instead and found my pub. I was so full of hope and excitement that I was almost bursting to get inside. My mood changed the moment I crossed the threshold. It was still very nice of course, but instead of the familiar surroundings I remembered I was horrified to see that many things had changed. Gone were the jukebox, the familiar décor and worst of all, the wonderful mirror. It had been removed from the back wall, which now was covered with some rather smart wallpaper and stylishly framed pictures. I could feel the tears of disappointment streaming down my face.
'Don't panic' I told myself and to steady my nerves, managed to ask the person at the bar for a drink.
I sat there for ages wondering what to do now.
Several drinks later I gave up and reluctantly made my way to my nearby budget hotel, found my room, and tried to get some sleep. After a fitful night I checked out of the hotel and forlornly went back for one more look at the place, before I returned home.
I now felt I had little hope of making contact with Sarah.
How wrong I was.
The moment I walked through the door I sensed something different and a familiar shiver ran down my spine. It reminded me of the first time I had sensed the presence of other beings in the basement of our shop back home in Darlington.
I bought my rum and coke and was walking towards the back of the establishment to take a seat near the place where the old mirror used to be, when suddenly everything changed. There was the wonderful mirror back in place again. Through it I could see that the room had grown darker and that the decor was now that of a bygone era. I could see a group of people reflected in the cloudy mirror glass,

and even though they were huddled together at a table with their backs to me, I knew immediately one was Sarah and guessed the other two would be Simon and Jimmy.
As soon as I called out her name Sarah gasped and turned her head. In a split second she had jumped to her feet and was embracing me. We both shed tears of relief. "I feared we would never see each other again," she sobbed.
"Same here," was my equally emotional reply.

The two young men at the table looked on in sheer amazement wondering whom this oddly dressed stranger that Simon's sister seemed to know so well might be. Sarah then proceeded to tell them as much of our circumstances as quickly and as gently as she could, as she could see how shaken they were.
I made a mental note to dress more suitably for the era if I ever got the chance to make this trip again. Denim jeans, Indian cotton kurta and leather jacket were hardly the usual mode of dress for a nineteenth century lady.
They were incredulous of the story she had to tell them at first, but eventually started to grasp the situation.
Simon recognised the perfume I was wearing as the same scent he had encountered once when he had experienced a strange sensation in the basement of 24, Blackwellgate, where he and his mother used to lodge.
I made him smile when I explained how that must have been the time when we somehow passed through each others bodies in the rather tight stairwell, due to us converging on the same small space (albeit in our different time zones), at the same moment. I spoke of how I had been able to glimpse him through the mists of time, as he and his mother approached me and how handsome I had thought he had looked. I also told him of my panic when I realised I could not get out of his way, followed by my relief that he had walked right through me with no ill effects to either of us. It was very hard for the two of them

to grasp it all, but once their initial disbelief had subsided, they took it very well.

The four of us talked for hours. After she had managed to tell me about the passing of Mrs. Thorpe, which had resulted in her losing access to our meeting place in the basement of number twenty four, Sarah and I could hardly get a word in edgeways as Simon and Jimmy had what seemed like endless questions to ask of me.
For my part I was so taken with their good looks and wonderful personalities, not to mention their obvious devotion to each other, that I shed a tear of joy. I was so happy that after the unhappiness and confusion they had experienced in earlier times, it looked certain they would now enjoy being together for the rest of their days.

The far too fleeting conversation I managed to have with Sarah on the other hand, revealed dramatic changes to her own situation. We wanted to talk in more depth about these but on this occasion time would just not allow it.
Hard as it was to do, I reluctantly now had to go, or I would miss my train back home. We two made a pact to be here at this same spot, at the same hour, in exactly seven days time. We just hoped and prayed that the merging of the time zones would work for us again.
Happily, they did and we were back in The Artichoke, exactly one week since our emotional re-union. This time it was just Sarah and I. We were pleased that there were few customers apart from us in the place on this occasion.
We decided to occupy a booth, so that we could have some privacy, as we had such a lot to talk about.
Over flagons of ale we told each other a lot more about what had happened during the months we had been apart. My news was not as life changing as hers turned out to be and sadly, given what she told me, it seemed as though this precious meeting might be the last we could enjoy. Even so, we tried to make the most of it and not to show how painful that felt to each of us.

Life must go on and we knew we both had to make our separate ways in our own different worlds.

Something unexpected had happened to Sarah. She was in love.

"I never thought I could ever feel this way," she excitedly told me.
"I'm so, so, happy for you. He must be really exceptional to be loved by someone as special as you are, Sarah," came my reply.
"He is, and I hope you can meet him someday," then her eyes lost their sparkle for a moment as she realised this would probably never happen.
I told her not to be sad, as I was just glad that at last she had found someone she could be happy with.

Up to now the lovely Sarah had resisted the advances of several suitors, preferring her independence to 'a suitable marriage', which was the route that young women of her times were expected to go down.
She was reaching her mid twenties and had been very happy with her life up to this point, so I don't think either of us could have ever foreseen this surprising development..

"Come on then, tell me about him," I said. That brought the joy back into her expression. She commenced to explain how the fates had caused her and the person she was certain was her true love to meet and what had subsequently happened to change the whole course of her life.
She added that she couldn't tell me the whole of the story as she had made someone a promise to keep certain elements of it to herself, but she did disclose quite enough for me to know that my friend (in spite of needing to clear one last huge hurdle), had finally found her true destiny.

I was stunned by what she told me and when she was finished I was very concerned for her safety. I just sat there for what seemed ages holding her close and wishing I could help her with what lay ahead. We finally had to tear ourselves away from one another and make our reluctant farewells. It was upsetting to us both, as it all seemed so final.
"Good luck and I will never forget you, Sarah," I whispered as I opened the door of 'The Artichoke,' which I could see in front of me and then closed the door of 'The Prince of Wales,' which I knew was behind me.
I had stepped back into the twenty first century, and was now headed off for Kings Cross Station to catch the train back home.

PART THREE

This story now needs to go back a few months in Sarah's world. Not knowing that she was soon to receive two miraculously timely visits from her friend from the future, Sarah Wheeler had by now given up hope of repeating the miracle of communicating with her ever again.
To try and take her mind off this loss she was often out and about exploring the streets and parks of London. She was hoping to find new characters and new inspiration for her stories. She knew that a young lady on her own shouldn't venture so far from the respectable area where she and her brother lodged with Jimmy Nicholson, but she had the inquisitive nature of a storyteller, so she did.
Just a short carriage ride from where they lived brought her to the edge of a very different world. A world where raggedy youngsters were seen begging or trying to sell trinkets and men and women who seemed to have lost hope sat idle on doorsteps or leaned against walls, occasionally swigging beer or gin from whichever bottle was in their hands.

She never wore extravagant clothes at any time, but sensibly; Sarah dressed even more plainly for her expeditions to these out of the way areas. It would not be wise to draw too much attention, so she blended in quite well. She always asked the carriage driver to wait at a spot she knew, so she felt reassured that if she encountered anything too unsettling she could find her way back quite quickly and hopefully no harm would have been done. She was upset to see that people were living in such obviously bad conditions and her main reason for being here was to gather material for some sort of written revelations, which might make these things known to the wider world. She hoped that perhaps by publicising their situations, she could maybe help to persuade the better off in society to make the lot of those who needed help a little more bearable.

On this particular day she had encountered a drunken couple as they staggered from a hostelry their arms entwined, and saw them head up a back street for obvious reasons. She also witnessed a fight between two youths over a coin they had both spotted lying on the cobbles. Worst of all she saw three very small thin children sitting forlornly outside a public house, perhaps waiting for their mother to come out of the place and hopefully take them home and feed them. She paused quickly and gave one of them a coin, hoping no one had seen her and may have been tempted to follow her in order to waylay her for more. These things had been enough for her for today and now her courage was failing, so she began to head back to where she had left the carriage. She took a short cut she had discovered that ran through an open patch of ground between some houses and what looked like a stable yard. The gates of the yard were open and not for the first time she sensed that someone was watching her. She was so busy looking over her shoulder to make sure she was not being followed that she tripped on a stone falling forward onto the cobbles. This resulted in her turning an ankle and hurting both her hands, which she had put out to save herself.

A young man appeared as if from no-where and hurried towards her. Panic welled up and her heart started to race, as she felt so vulnerable lying there alone on the ground in this deserted place. Clutching on tightly to the little velvet drawstring bag that she carried on her wrist, she had struggled to her knees by now and was trying to get up, but the damaged ankle wouldn't quite support her. The stranger looked concerned, knelt down at her side and in a pleasant West Country accent asked if she was hurt. "Just scraped my hands a bit and can't seem to get up," she heard herself reply.
Sarah couldn't help noticing that the stranger's brown eyes were very beguiling and currently bore a concerned expression, but she still worried that she may have got herself into a tricky situation.
As he helped her back up she thanked him, adding that she was just a bit shaken but no real harm had been done. He seemed pleased at that.
"I know you're not lost Miss as I've seen you here before, but I know most of the lasses from around these parts by name and I don't know you?"
"Oh, I'm Sarah" she shyly replied and immediately felt stupid for telling him her name.
The truth was that she felt weak at the knees in the close proximity of this handsome stranger, whose strong arms had just lifted her back onto her feet and that was not like her at all.
Thankfully the ankle held firm, so Sarah began to limp off saying, "I must go as I need to meet with someone!" He called after her, "well my name is Locryn" and added, "perhaps I will see you here again?"
She smiled over her shoulder at him and proceeded on her way.
Once back in the safety of the carriage she asked the driver to take her home and all the way back her heart was still beating so rapidly she almost feared it would leap from her chest.

Over the days that followed the ankle recovered and Sarah decided to venture out again. She avoided going back to the place where she had met Locryn at first but, eventually, in spite of trying to resist the temptation, on one of her trips she found herself heading there.

This time there was a lot of noise coming from the yard and a several horse drawn carts were waiting in the alley outside and when she saw the drivers of these carts loading them up with barrels, she realised this place must be part of a brewery.

She didn't catch sight of the young man who had often occupied her thoughts since her last visit here, but at least now she knew a little more about him.

Wrapped up warmly, as the weather had turned quite cold, a few weeks later Sarah was again drawn to that place. Turning into the alley she saw that on this occasion all was quiet. The nearer she drew to the yard the more nervous she felt. If by chance he was around the lad might not remember her and she would feel foolish for coming here. He might not even work at this job any longer and if so she would probably never see him again.

He was there, however, and her heart skipped a beat when she saw the look of pleasure on his face when he caught sight of her. She'd decided he was a few years younger than herself and that gave her a little more confidence too.

After greeting her and enquiring about her ankle, Locryn invited her inside, telling her that it was just his mother, himself and a couple of young lads who were around today, as everyone else was away attending to other business. Sarah was unsure whether to accept at first, but felt bolder when she head a female voice call out, "Locryn, there's hot tea if you want it!"

"My friend here could do with one too," he called back.

Locryn's mother didn't query that, which made Sarah wonder if bringing strange girls in to sample her tea was a regular occurrence. 'Heavens above, I think I may be jealous,' thought Sarah.

Anyway, just then a very striking looking woman appeared. This dark haired lady introduced herself as Vyvyan and handed each of them a nice porcelain cup full to the brim of a delicious hot brew. She then went off to take two, slightly more sturdy cups, to the others who were working at the other side of the yard.

Sarah silently chided herself for allowing that twinge of jealousy to surface. That was not like her at all. After all she hardly knew this boy, but somehow she sensed then and there that their destinies would one day be entwined.

Sarah and Locryn stood sipping their tea in awkward silence at first until Sarah enquired, "so, what do you and your mother do around here?"

"I look after the yard and the horses and we're sort of caretakers here too," was his reply.

"Allow me to show you around," he added.

They did a tour of the yard, which was much larger than it seemed from the outside. There were stalls for half a dozen or so horses, a hay store, an area where several carts were parked up under cover and she also glimpsed a boxing ring. The other lads, having finished their tea, were busy sweeping up outside the doors of a large building, which took up the whole of one side of this place.

"That's the back of the brewery and we have rooms next to the offices upstairs in there," he told her. "The front of the brewery faces onto Cobden Square."

Trying to keep the conversation going, Sarah enquired, "Is this a good place to work?"

Locryn's face became serious as he told her, "Only in some ways. Don't think I'm not grateful for my job here with the animals and the deliveries but I very much dislike some of the other things that go on!"

She hoped he would continue to explain what he meant but could see that he felt he had said enough, so instead she just asked, "If it's that bad, why do you stay?"

His expression brightened again.

"Perhaps because I knew that one day you would turn up here," he teased.

Then blushing slightly at his own boldness, he changed the subject, "Come and see the horses…"

With a little thrill of excitement, Sarah willingly headed off with him in the direction of the stables.
That was to be the first of many meetings between these two and they always took place on the days when the yard was quiet and Jed, the owner's son was busy elsewhere, attending to these other mysterious business tasks that had been mentioned.
As time went by she picked up a few more insights into what went on and started to understand why the owner's son was often absent.

A big sign hung over the front door of the brewery proudly proclaiming that this was 'Jackson's Brewery' and officially in charge of it all was Jacob Jackson, the shrewd head of the clan, who, in addition to building up and running this legitimate and respected business, also used to have fingers in many other pies. Some linked to the London underworld. These included dogfights, cockfights, bare knuckle fighting and gambling.
Nowadays, as he was getting on in years, Jackson senior had lost his appetite for that kind of thing and mainly took care of the brewery side of it all.
He had been born into poverty and had only been able to rise to his present position of power by cutting a few corners in the past and the habit had stuck. His desire for dealing with these more questionable enterprises had faded however, so now his son, Jed, handled that side of things and had taken it to whole new levels.
Jacob was already married to a lady named Anne (Jed's mother), but she suffered from ill health. He took care of her very well but due to her delicate state they were now husband and wife in name only. So when he met and developed a fancy for a young widow called Vyvyan, who had quite recently arrived in London from her native Cornwall, his lawful wife had no objections.

Vyvyan not only liked this gentleman but she also had a young son (Locryn) to bring up, so she was happy to accept his advances and his offer of help.

As well as being darkly beautiful Vyvyan was also something of a mystic (in fact it was said that she was a Cornish witch), and that rumour was what had drawn Jacob to her in the first place. Like many of his kind who had suffered obstacles on his way to the top, he was very superstitious.

This couple got on famously with each other, shared mutual needs and their relationship suited them both very well.

He liked to keep her close, almost like a lucky charm, so eventually although he officially resided at the big house he owned nearby, with his wife and son, he set her and her child up in very nice rooms at the brewery, where he would frequently stay overnight. Then when her boy grew old enough Jacob gave him employment at the stables caring for the brewery's delivery horses. The lad had been doing this job, very satisfactorily, ever since.

Sarah learned all this from her talks with Locryn.

Over the course of their meetings he also told her to be very wary of their benefactor's son, Jed Jackson, who, because of his cruel nature was known behind his back as "Big Nasty".

When she heard this nickname for the first time, Sarah wanted to giggle, but the look on Locryn's face stopped her. He was deadly serious and told her, "this person is dangerous and his name says it all. He is big, he is nasty and he is ruthless. He will stop at nothing and he takes pleasure in causing misery to and crushing the spirit out of others. I often wish he didn't exist. His father is the only one who can come near to controlling him and even he struggles.

This caused Sarah to say, "I hope you don't mind me asking this, but what happened to your own father?"

"I never knew him. I was told he passed away just before I was born," came the sad reply.

Jed Jackson was indeed a nasty piece of work, but even though she had usurped his own mother in his father's bed, he was always careful around Vyvyan. Just like his father he was extremely superstitious and he believed in and also feared her powers. At first, he even reluctantly tolerated her son being around and complied when she insisted that Locryn was not to be involved in any of the firm's shady dealings.
This situation changed as Vyvyan's boy got older.
Jed came to realise that his father was beginning to think of Locryn as a second son and that made him nervous. He started to take every opportunity to belittle the lad. He'd call him a "mother's boy" and much worse in front of the other workers in the hope of goading him into a confrontation, which the older and much stronger man knew he would win. Locryn, was no coward but he was also clever enough to diffuse these situations with a witty retort. This annoyed Jed even more but he never let it show.

Steadily and naturally Sarah and Locryn drew closer and closer together. Their first kiss was a revelation. It was shy, passionate, sweet and tender all at the same time and they repeated this delicious experience as often as they possibly could. Sarah knew he was not short of female admirers, but since they had met he only had eyes for her.
For her part, Sarah had never even dreamed that such powerful feelings were possible. These emotions were beyond her own or anyone else's control. For the first time ever she was in love.
An exquisite shiver of pleasure would run through her whole body every time she met with Locryn. She thrilled at the way his whole face lit up at the sight of her and the mere touch of his hand on hers triggered exquisite flashes of pleasure which sent her weak at the knees.
When they were apart he was constantly on her mind.

Their mutual attraction was so strong that she never doubted he felt the same way, so it came as no surprise when he finally plucked up the courage to put into words how much he cared.
Now they both knew this was real and would change their lives forever

Then one fateful day something happened which put their happiness and safety under threat.
Sarah came face to face with the infamous Jed Jackson, Big Nasty himself!
The aura surrounding the person before her seemed to suck the energy from her body. He was an overwhelming man standing over six feet tall and obviously in the prime of life. He had shaved all the hair off his head, no doubt to make himself appear even more intimidating to others than he already was, but had kept a fierce red beard. His face might have been classed as handsome had it not been for the arrogant twist of his lips and the cold expression in his hard steely blue eyes.
She could see that Jed was extremely well muscled as he was stripped to the waist and dripping with sweat having just been sparring with one of his fighters in the ring, to keep his hand in. The fight had ended with a resounding win for him, of course, so he was in a reasonably good mood.
His expression changed at the sight of Sarah. He didn't like strangers on the premises, even if they were as pretty as this one was.
Grabbing her by the arm he bent forward until his face was almost touching hers.
She could feel his breath on her cheek as he growled, "Who are you then, Missy?"
"A friend of Vyvyan's," was her startled reply. She was quick enough not to mention Locryn's name at this point.
At this his eyes widened a little with surprised interest.

"Not the usual kind of wench we get around here," he observed and to her horror he licked all down one side of her face with his hot raspy tongue, before stepping away and letting go of her arm
"You taste good. I might even let you call to see her again," he told her as he strode off to cool down.
As soon as he was out of sight Sarah went to find Vyvyan and told her about this troubling development.
With Vyvyan to vouch for her, Sarah kept on visiting the yard but she knew that now she was being watched much of the time.
Jed soon realised that the main reason she came to the premises was, in fact, to spend time with Locryn and began taking an unhealthy interest in her with the intention of provoking trouble.
Big Nasty now seemed to be present at the yard a lot more frequently.
If he were around he would often intercept Sarah as soon as she arrived and proceed to make lewd suggestions. She was terrified that Locryn might overhear him and would challenge him.
Fortunately Vyvyan always managed to appear just at the right moment in order to prevent things going too far.
Neither of the women in his life told Locryn about the harassment Sarah was suffering for fear of what might happen if he knew, but it got to the point where Sarah decided it would be safer for everyone concerned if she tried to arrange a different place to see her true love.
How she was going to manage to do this without stirring up trouble was another matter of course. Eventually, in order to give her time to find a solution, she made an excuse to Locryn about having to go away for a while to attend to a family matter. Although it nearly broke both their hearts she stopped going to Jackson's Brewery for a while. She secretly let Vyvyan know where to get in touch with her should the need arise and only resumed her visits when she received some very sad news from her about Jacob Jackson.

PART FOUR

Jacob's health had deteriorated over the last few months and his physician had told him that without Vyvyan's care he would have probably been bed-ridden or worse by now. He added that even in spite of her efforts the prospect was not good. There was not much that could be done and he advised that Jacob should put his affairs in order. When Vyvyan heard this she wept and made up one of her potions for him, to at least ease his physical pain.
The Cornish lady was genuinely sad about Jacob's illness and also very worried for Locryn. She didn't need psychic powers to realise that when the day came that Jacob was no longer around to control things, the conflict between his son and her own would finally come to a head.
She decided that something must be done to avert this catastrophe, so she started to make plans.
She would, however, need to include Sarah in this in order for her scheme to succeed.
A private meeting was arranged.

Vyvyan warned Sarah in advance that she planned to use magic to help them with what lay ahead.

That evening the two of them met at the home of a friend of Vyvyan's who also practised The Craft.
Sarah was trembling as she approached the ornate black wrought iron gate guarding this place, but thankfully Vyvyan was there to meet her. They closed the gate behind them and headed up a short footpath to the house itself and on knocking were welcomed inside by a most charming elderly gentleman. Once inside the entrance hall introductions were made and their host ushered them down into the basement, which had already been prepared for the night's activities to take place.

Then he left them alone to do what was necessary to work this most dangerous situation out.

There were several ornate silver framed mirrors on the walls; a large pentagram marked out on the floor and lighted candles everywhere. The flames from the candles were reflected in the mirrors and the place seemed as if it were on fire.

Sarah felt very nervous. She knew how dangerous their situation was, so she tried to stay calm and concentrate, but she thought she was about to faint.

She could hear Vyvyan's voice as if from a distance, saying, "I sense that you have strengths of your own which we are going to need to tap into if we are going to foil Jed Jackson's evil intentions. In order to do this the two of us must pool our resources and become even closer than we are now."

"To test our capacity for trust I am going to tell you something that I have never revealed to anyone else. It is a secret that my son must never know. First, however, you need to share with me the secret I know you carry with you too, in order to seal our deal."

Sarah's head was spinning. How on earth could Vyvyan know of her secret, she wondered. Then she reminded herself that Vyvyan knew many hidden things. So, for the first time ever, up to that point in her life, she found herself relating the details of her journeys across time to another person. Vyvyan took these revelations all in her stride and nodded understandingly. She observed that Sarah was lucky to have had such special experiences. Then she commenced to keep her side of the pact. "I want you to know that Locryn's father is not dead. I used my powers to send him away shortly after my boy was born," she told the girl.

Vyvyan let that sink in, then continued, "I had good reason for doing this as if I hadn't he would have destroyed us all. He became afflicted by a madness, which I couldn't cure. I consulted the crystal and saw what lay ahead for him, for me and for our child and I was filled with dread.

If I hadn't done what I did, I believe there would have been terrible consequences for us all and I could not let that happen."

"After the spell wore off, he took up with some other poor unfortunate female and let us be for many years," she then continued, "but when Locryn was almost twelve years old he came back to claim him, not from love but so that he could punish me. That is when I fled to London, as I feared for our safety."

Although Sarah was prepared to do whatever she could to help, she still had to ask, "doesn't your son have a right to know his father is alive?" Vyvyan forcefully replied, "NO, because I fear it would make him want to find him and my husband is a madman who would lead him to his death." She then added. "I hope this honesty shows the high regard I have for you and how much I trust you to make my son happy?"

"Now, are you prepared to keep this between us?"

"If it is for the good of us all, especially Locryn, then yes I can keep this secret," Sarah pledged. "We will speak of it no more. I hate to keep anything from Locryn, but I do believe that you foresaw monstrous things and acted for the best. Thank you for trusting me and I promise that this knowledge is safe with me!"

With that assurance the two of them bonded.

They now had more pressing dangers to deal with.

Vyvyan was now keen to continue, "I don't need my visions to see that Jed Jackson lusts after you and hates my son, but I do need them to see more exactly the evils he has on his mind!

With that she sat down at a small round table and asked Sarah to sit opposite her. She uncovered a crystal ball which had been lying on the table hidden by a velvet cloth and placed it in Sarah's cupped hands. Next she wrapped her own hands around Sarah's and thus entwined they gazed together into the magical sphere.

Through the mist, which was clouding the ball, the cold blue eyes of Jed Jackson appeared, almost filling the whole space within it. As they both looked into those eyes it was possible to access his murderous thoughts. "He plans to defile you in the presence of my son in order to provoke a reaction which will end in Locryn's death, but he won't make his move until his father's suffering is over and he is laid to rest," gasped Vyvyan.
"Sadly I don't think that will be long as Jacob gets weaker every day."

More revelations of Jed's cruelty and depravity followed, until they could bear it no longer...
Sarah cried out in shocked disgust and they both let go of the ball simultaneously. It rolled over the table, until Vyvyan recovered enough to put a hand out to steady it just before it reached the edge. They were both trembling due to the wickedness they had seen. They embraced one another for comfort until this shaking had stopped. The window to Jed's black soul had been revealed and they had seen the worst.
Vyvyan now knew the very hour that he would strike and it was to be on the day that Jacob would be laid to rest

She was tempted to send Jed straight to hell, right there and then, as she knew she could have summoned up the power to achieve this. She held back however, because deserving as an individual might be of such a fate, she had vowed never use her considerable gifts to take the life of another human being. That ultimate deed would require her to sacrifice her own soul and would have only unleashed more darkness into the world.

Sarah felt very afraid, "we may have very little time left then. Just tell me what you think can be done and I will do it."
"You both need to get away," whispered the Cornish witch.
Sarah agreed, "but how will we persuade Locryn, he won't want to run away, he will want to stay and fight?"

"If the fates had decreed that he would be the victor in all of this I would not have intervened, but as you have seen there is too much against him. There is no doubt in my mind that leaving here is the only way, Sarah, and although I don't like to practice my Craft on my own flesh and blood, I will do whatever it takes to convince him to do that."
"Sarah's next question was, "What about you when we are gone?" Vyvyan looked at her with those compelling grey/green eyes of hers and stated, "I'm coming with you!!!"

They worked out the plan in detail so that both would know where to be and what to do when the time came, and then their business concluded, they prepared to leave. The crystal ball was carefully wrapped up again and after snuffing out all of the candles, apart from the one they carried with them to light their way back up the stairs, they said their thanks to the owner of this safe house and went their separate ways…

Thankfully Sarah had made certain that Jed Jackson had never been able to have her followed back to the place where she lodged, so she had no fears for her brother's and Jimmy's safety once she was gone. Being as close as these three were, however, they needed to know the truth of the situation so that they wouldn't worry about her when she had to leave. They were worried of course when she told them the whole story, but they could see how determined she was and asked how they could help. She threw her arms around them and kissed them both in turn, insisting, "It's better if Vyvyan and I do this alone as I would only fret if you two got involved!"
Simon and Jimmy reluctantly agreed, but as they both loved her dearly they couldn't help but be fearful until the deed had been safely done.
"I'll write when I get as far away as is needed," she told them and they had to make do with that.
To cheer them up Sarah suggested they all go to The Artichoke and drink to success. That was the very day that her dear friend from the

future had also decided to visit that place. So, as fate would have it, once again at a time of great stress their paths converged and these two time travellers were able to spend precious hours in one another's company.

PART FIVE

Jacob Jackson slipped away in the arms of his beloved Vyvyan. She prayed to The Goddess this was not just an end but also a beginning.

She had placed a spell on her son to ensure he would comply with whatever she or Sarah directed him to do when the time came. The escape plan was in place and would be put into action whilst Joseph's wake was in progress. They were relying on the fact that Jed, (or Big Nasty as they now referred to him all the time), would be too occupied socialising with family and friends, not to mention finalising his plan to get rid of Locryn once and for all, to notice that they had slipped away.

Once he realised they had gone Vyvyan guessed that Big Nasty would assume she and Locryn had returned by road to Cornwall taking Sarah with them, but in fact they were going to head North by train. Even though he had never discovered that Sarah was originally from Darlington, they decided not to make that town their destination. They needed somewhere much smaller and quieter to hide.
Finally Sarah came up with the ideal place, a small town called Bedale, which she knew of and liked.

They had money, they had the time and tickets for the train and a means of quickly getting to the station. They would make that journey hidden under a tarpaulin, in a horse drawn cart, that Vyvyan's friend (the male witch who had kindly let them use his house to hatch their plan), would drive.

Vyvyan had slipped a powerful but temporary paralysis potion into the drinks she had sent to the two burley men who had been tasked with standing guard at the gates to the yard. They were there with strict instructions from Jed to detain anyone who tried to enter or leave whilst the wake was in progress (especially Locryn or Sarah), so they needed to be rendered inactive.

All they had to do now was to keep their nerve and make this happen, and it did…

Big Nasty's rage when he realised they had gone was beyond terrifying. His bloodcurdling roar of anger could be heard from streets away.
He lashed out viciously at his henchmen for not being more vigilant, smashed up everything in the rooms that his father had provided for his mistress and her son at the brewery and was furious with himself for underestimating Vyvyan, whom he realised must have used her spells to save her son and the wench.
It was all to no avail, as they were long gone and he had no idea where.

PART SIX

The three escapees arrived tired, drained but relieved at Darlington station. They spent the night at Chorley Hall where they were welcome guests. The next day they explained as much as they could about what had happened, to Mrs Nicholson (Sarah's mentor and Jimmy Nicholson's mother) and Sarah's own mother, Barbara (who was now Mrs Nicholson's companion). The two ladies were shocked but very glad that Sarah and her companions were now safe.
Then they hired a coach and set off for Bedale.
Once they had reached this pretty market town they found rooms at a guesthouse, which they made their base camp whilst they looked for somewhere more permanent to live.

After the ordeals of recent times they all agreed that it would be best to find a quiet place where, for a while at least, they could escape from the rest of the world and gather their thoughts, after the traumatic events they had just lived through.
That place presented itself to them in what seemed like no time at all. When they enquired of the lady who owned the guesthouse whether she knew of any properties to rent in the area, she told them that a relative of hers had recently passed away leaving her a tiny cottage with a plot of land attached. This place was a few miles out of Bedale in a small hamlet called Burrill.
It sounded ideal.
A deal was struck to rent it unseen. The next day they bought some provisions, loaded their few belongings onto a cart which their landlady had commissioned for the purpose, and instructed the driver to take them to their new home deep in the North Yorkshire countryside.

PART SEVEN

Many years had passed since Sarah, Locryn and Vyvyan had fled from London and made their home in the country.
At first, once the spell had worn off, Locryn had wanted to go straight back to London and confront Big Nasty, but the women talked him out of it.
"Don't risk the freedom we have achieved and put us all in danger again, just to settle an old score with that monster," pleaded his mother.
Sarah just said, "We have all we need here and knowing that we outwitted him and are now enjoying the kind of happiness that he can never have, is punishment enough for Jed Jackson!"

He finally saw the wisdom of their words and agreed they were right.

The two young lovers were now free to build a happy life together. Sarah had given up quite a lot to run away with her love, but she had not one doubt in her head that it had been worth it.
They married at the church in Bedale and now Sarah and Locryn would face the world together as man and wife.

In 1880 Sarah gave birth to George (which had been Locryn's father's name). Vyvyan did not object to her grandson's name at all, as she felt that she owed Locryn the right to commemorate his absent father in this way.
Then four years later Barbara (named after Sarah's own mother) came along to complete their family.

By now they had bought the tiny cottage, which they had originally rented and made some improvements to it.
Life for each and every one of them was very good.

Sarah still wrote stories, but just for her own pleasure and to amuse her children now. She did not make her work public any longer for fear of attracting unwanted publicity.

Locryn had found a job on a nearby farm, where he worked hard and was held in high esteem. The owners, being childless, came to treat him as if he were their own son.

Vyvyan, although still a very good looking woman, declared there would be no more men in her life now that Jacob was gone and was content with things exactly as they were. She delighted in cooking them all delicious meals, doted on her grandchildren and performed the odd helpful spell for people living nearby in exchange for such things as fresh eggs or garden produce. She did not consciously broadcast the fact that she had mystical gifts, but these things have a habit of getting around.

They lived modestly within their means and got along just fine.
They didn't miss London at all and were very, very happy.

Regular trips to Darlington were made in order to visit Eleanor
Nicholson and Sarah's mother, Barbara Wheeler.
Whilst there they would attend to any banking business Sarah had
and also indulge in a little bit of shopping. She always managed to
linger for a while outside number 24 Blackwellgate, in the hope of
connecting with her friend from the future, but sadly that never
happened.
They tried to time these visits to coincide with trips home made by
Simon and Jimmy too, as Sarah loved these people very much and
they loved her in return.

The children were growing up now and Mrs Nicholson and Mrs
Wheeler were growing older.
1890 was a very sad year for them all as first Sarah's mother passed
away and then shortly after her Eleanor Nicholson also died.
Sarah was there to comfort them both in their final hours.
The Hall was sold and most of the proceeds went to Eleanor's son,
Jimmy, but she also made provision in her will for her beloved Sarah,
(who had helped her so much in her difficult earlier life), to receive a
yearly annuity for the rest of her days.
The funeral services for both these highly regarded women, one
Quaker and one High Church, were very different, but both were
celebrations of lives well led.
To cap a terrible year off they suddenly also lost Vyvyan in rather
puzzling circumstances.
She had not shown any signs of illness and yet one day she just didn't
get up from her bed. When Sarah went to check on her she found her
lying with a peaceful expression on her face and a photograph of their
little family clutched to her heart. On trying to wake her she was
horrified to discover that she was cold and still and now at rest.

Sarah couldn't help wondering if she had sacrificed her own life in place of one of theirs, as she remembered that after their earlier two losses, Vyvyan had taken her aside saying very seriously, "Death often comes in threes, but I will ensure that you and yours are safe, my dear!"
A sadness hung over Sarah and Locryn for a long time afterwards, but knowing that their loved one would want them to get on with things, eventually they managed to return to something like normality.
From then onwards they treasured each other even more than before, if that were possible.

Now that their mother's were gone Simon and Jimmy didn't visit Darlington as often as they used to before. The family home had now been sold and their busy lives and jobs were firmly based in London. Of course they did both still make the trip, at least once a year, to keep in contact with Sarah and her family, but they always wrote ahead to warn them that they were coming.
This is why it was a great surprise when one day, out of the blue, Jimmy arrived at the door of the cottage unannounced.
He was not alone, but it wasn't Simon he had with him, it was a dark haired lad of about eighteen years old.
Jimmy introduced the stranger saying, "Sarah, this is my relative from Spain, Roderigo and I have a big favour to ask of you and your family, concerning him?"
Sarah kissed Jimmy on the cheek and clasped Roderigo by the hands in welcome, as she invited them both inside.
She was intrigued as to why this Spanish boy was here.
Sarah remembered that Jimmy's own grandmother had been Spanish and realised that he would, of course, have family in that country. It turned out that Jimmy's cousin in Spain, who was also called Roderigo (a name which in Spanish means notable leader), was involved in some sort of dangerous political conflict with certain people in the turbulent Spanish Government and feared that he and his family may be put under arrest or worse. For this reason he had arranged for his

son to be smuggled out of their own country and sent to England for the sake of the boys safety.
As Roderigo junior was here in secret, Jimmy had thought that in case Spanish spies who knew he had relations in London had followed him, it was wise to bring him somewhere quiet until things had hopefully calmed down.
"Can he lodge here for a while please, Sarah? I'm afraid I don't know exactly how long his stay will have to be!?"
"I'll have to ask my husband of course," she told him, and then added, "I don't think Locryn will object as we know very well what it is like to be fugitives!"
As expected, when he came home, Locryn agreed. .
Jimmy slept that night on their kitchen sofa and then set off to return to London the next day, leaving his cousin's son in their care.

PART EIGHT

Roderigo stayed for several weeks and everyone took to this good looking boy, but they could see he worried a lot about the struggles his father had to deal with in Spain. One day he received a letter from his own country, the contents of which made his normally pleasant disposition turn dark and brooding and they all knew he must have had bad news concerning the situation at home.
One fateful morning when Locryn went to wake him, he had gone. They worried for his safety. A young lad with a foreign accent travelling alone in a strange country could get lost or suffer violence at the hands of rowdies.
They were all very upset, but not so much as their daughter was. The girl was in floods of tears, which nothing and nobody could stop. Sarah held her daughter close and stroked her hair saying, "Shush, shush, you will make yourself ill if this goes on much longer," but Barbara still wept uncontrollably. "We will not be angry with you my love, but did you know that Roderigo planned on leaving?"

"Yes, but he has promised me that he will come back," she sobbed. Time went by and there was no news, but the reason for Barbara's tears soon became clear. Their girl was with child and, of course, it was the absent Roderigo's child.

Sarah knew what a scandal a baby born out of wedlock would cause, as girls who were unmarried mothers were considered ruined and found it hard to make their way in life.

Not wanting that for their daughter, Sarah and Locryn decided that if there was no chance of the boy she loved coming back to make things right, after the birth they would bring the child up as their own. They also offered to pay for the girl to go away to college to study music, which had long been her ambition.

At first Barbara wasn't sure, as she still hoped that Roderigo would return and they would be married.

Then one dark day they received the news from London that having somehow made his way back to Jimmy's house the boy had insisted on going to Spain to be at his father's side and now both had been reported missing, believed dead.

Barbara was inconsolable at first, but with support from her parents she reluctantly acquiesced to their suggestions about her future.

A few months later she gave birth. The little boy stayed with his grandparents and his mother moved away to follow her childhood dream of training to be a pianist.

Before she left she saw her child christened Rupert.

Little Rupert was brought up by his grandma and granddad and was greatly loved. He was a beautiful, intelligent little chap and the apple of Sarah's eye. He also had a good friend in his Uncle George who the boy looked up to and admired.

Everyone noticed that just like his mother before him, he had inherited his granddad Locryn's wonderful brown eyes.

Barbara got her music degree and threw herself into teaching piano at first and then got taken on by a touring theatrical show.

After a long time spent grieving she found love again with an admirer she had met whilst on tour, who asked her to marry him and return North to be nearer to both their families.
Her new husband wanted to start a family of their own, so her love child stayed with his grandparents, whilst she made a new life for herself, and no one could really blame her.

Life went on as normal for the four members of this family who remained at the cottage in Burrill, and together they enjoyed great happiness.
Sarah and Rupert had formed a real bond and she would refer to him as, "My little man!"
The years passed by and the child grew up to be very handsome. When he was old enough, Sarah's 'little man' became an army cadet. He looked very smart in his uniform.
Then once again, major tragedy struck and this time with a most heartbreaking result.
Locryn contracted tuberculosis and faded away.
Sarah was a very strong person but this cruel loss of the love of her life rocked her to her very core. She now became ill herself. Grief overtook her. She wouldn't eat and hardly slept at all for weeks on end and became so thin that the people who loved her feared that she would soon join her adored husband.
Then one day she woke from one of her rare slumbers and saw young Rupert sobbing his heart out at the foot of her bed and that sight finally got through to her.
The realisation dawned that for the sake of their remaining family, life after Locryn's death must go on.
Her loving son George and charismatic grandson Rupert stayed by her side and thanks to her two boys, she gradually regained her health. They all knew, however, that as much as she loved them, she was now in deep mourning and her life would never be quite the same again.

She did take pleasure in watching George and Rupert's progress through their lives, however, and soon they both began to 'spread their wings'!

After years of being a bachelor, to every one's surprise, George, courted and married a pretty girl called Ada, who was much younger than he was himself and together they opened a grocery and provisions shop in the village.

Rupert, with his startling good looks and engaging personality found himself to be very popular with everyone he met and got lots of attention from the opposite sex too.

He grew restless, as young men do, however, and much as he didn't want to leave his grandmother on her own he knew he would need to leave this small village one day and at least she had George and Ada nearby. His superior in The Cadets was a Scotsman whom he regarded as a father figure. These two would talk for hours about Scotland and great battles, adventures and such. The boy was a dreamer and he fell in love with the romantic idea of joining a Scottish regiment called
The Black Watch.
Sorry though she was to see him leave his grandmother made it possible for him to realise this dream. He promised to come back often when he was on leave and of course he kept his word.
This departure had been made easier for him due to the fact that by now George had sold up at the shop and returned to the cottage where he had been born, to live with his mother. Sadly his marriage had broken down even though he and his young wife had now got a lovely little daughter. The decision to part had mainly been due to their age differences, so they had agreed amicably, to go their separate ways. They both knew it was best that their baby went with her mother.

Rupert promised his adored Grandma that he would come back to see her and his uncle George often, and he kept his word.

How handsome he looked when he would return to visit wearing the regimental kilt, and what a stir he caused amongst the ladies of the area.

It was on one of these visits that he and a boyhood friend, Bobby Hutch (Hutchinson), decided to go to a popular annual event known as Eppleby Gala and that is where he met his future wife.

These boys caused quite a flurry of excitement when they walked into the village hall where there was a dance going on. This was mainly due to the fact that Rupert was wearing his kilt. They looked around and Rupert's eyes alighted on a tall slender young lady who stood out from the crowd.

"See that little blonde over there," he whispered to Bobby. "I'm going to ask her for a dance."

That was it. Love at first sight.

The girl and boy danced all evening. They whirled around the floor as if in a magical fairy tale. Her fair wavy hair was tumbling around her pretty face and his heart melting dark brown eyes were smiling just for her.

Irene's dainty feet seemed hardly to touch the ground and Rupert's tartan kilt swung jauntily, as they danced around the floor (to the great delight of all the female's present).

They were the envy of all the people in the room that night and their destiny was set.

Irene was a tenant farmer's daughter. Her mother and father were called Tom and Annie and her brother was named Humphrey.

When they heard that their daughter wanted to get married to this total stranger, "as soon as possible," they said, "NO!"

She was not even eighteen years old after all.

She nagged and nagged them about it and when they wouldn't give their consent, she tried to elope to Gretna Green with Rupert, but was prevented when Humphrey discovered her plan and told their parents. They then tried to send her away to the South of England to train as a nurse, but she wouldn't go. Finally, after she had gone with Rupert to the registry office in Yarm and tried to forge her father's signature on a consent form to enable them to marry there, they realised she would not be put off and gave in to this young couples wishes.

The marriage took place and finally she was happy.

"I always wanted to marry a man that every other girl wanted, and now I have," she declared.

Rupert went back to his regiment but he had not been away long before a message came saying that Irene had a thyroid problem and needed an urgent operation. The family didn't have much money so her brother Humph had asked his employer, at the haulage firm he worked for, to lend him two months wages in advance. He promised his boss that he would work this debt off and knowing the reason for which the money was needed, Mr Cracknell agreed. Humphrey used this money to pay for his sister's surgery to be done. Irene went into hospital and underwent the operation. She may have been mentally feisty she wasn't the strongest of girls physically and whilst she was having the operation something went wrong and she nearly died.

Word was sent to her young husband that he should come home immediately. Irene was very poorly and so Rupert asked for extended leave from The Black Watch, on compassionate grounds, in order to stay at her side.

He stayed close until she somehow got through the worst and gradually her health returned. After her illness he never went back to his regiment, as he didn't want them to be parted again, so his father-in-law Tom Fishburn, bought him out.

Once he was certain she would be able to manage without him he then joined a more local regiment, The Green Howards, where he did very well and soon became a corporal.

In 1939 World War Two broke out.

Because he was a professional soldier himself, Rupert was immediately assigned to training new recruits.

First of all he was stationed at Aske Hall where he became a very useful NCO. Soon he rose to the rank of Sergeant. The war rumbled on and he got transferred to Shrewsbury, but was never sent abroad as he was more valuable to the army here in his own country. Irene's parents had given up farming and moved to a house in Orchard Road, Darlington by now. As Rupert was now stationed so far away, Irene went with them. On the occasions when he managed to get leave, Rupert too stayed with them there and that is where, one late December day, their only child was born.

There was much squabbling about what to name the little girl. Irene's mam, Annie, wanted Olwyn after a favourite cousin. Rupert was having none of that. Then she suggested, Hazel, but he told her that when she went to school with that name, the other kids might call her nutty. It was Irene, weak as she was from her long labour, who turning to her husband came up with the solution. Why don't we call her Beryl, as you always say how much you admire that actress, Beryl Ord and also it sounds a bit like Burrill, where you were so happy growing up.

So the perfect name was agreed. Annie still pushed to have the name Olwyn included and Beryl as a middle name. Again Rupert resisted, pointing out that, as her birthday was so near to Christmas, the combination of those two names could lead to her being known as Ollie Berry. Annie at last gave up and Irene and Rupert got their way. Their child would have one first name only. The new mother took a while to recover from the birth. As soon as Irene was well enough, she and Rupert decided that they had a very important trip to make. So, before they had their daughter christened they agreed they should take the baby to Burrill, to meet her great grandmother and get her blessing.

Once the winter weather had picked up enough for them to travel, that is what they did.

It was in the January of 1944 that this family of three drove to Burrill in a car borrowed from Irene's brother, Humphrey. They arrived early in the afternoon, parked the vehicle in the lane outside, opened the wicket gate, went up the little path and knocked on the cottage door. Rupert's grandmother, Sarah, opened the door and her eyes lit up at the sight of her visitors. The love between her and her grandson was palpable.

PART NINE

Here was I, stuck in the twenty first century, not knowing what had happened to the dear friend I had lost contact with at a most crucial period in her life. I fretted dreadfully about her, as I sensed it was important to us both that I found out if she had overcome the dangers she was about to face when I last saw her.
Regression therapy was not something I had ever contemplated, as I was terrified of being hypnotised after a bad experience in my childhood. Nevertheless, re-occurring dreams, which I'd been experiencing lately, seemed to suggest that clues to my connection with Sarah lay buried in my own past. I therefore decided I must try this (to me at least), scary technique, if I truly wanted to know the truth.
Once again I got in touch with Mrs Sangster (the medium who had helped me so much in earlier times when I had first made contact with Sarah).
She told me that what I needed to undergo was present life regression, rather than past life regression. She said she knew an excellent practitioner who could help me remember things which were buried in my consciousness and beyond my own reach.
I trusted Mrs Sangster as she had never let me down, so nervous as I was, I rang Kenneth Doyle, the therapist she had suggested. Several times before the day we had arranged to meet for the session I experienced panic attacks and almost cancelled my appointment, but I didn't do it as this was too important to me to pull out now. Mrs Sangster said she would come along to the session to give me some support and that made me feel a bit better about the whole thing.

It was decided that my regression should take place in the basement of 24, Blackwellgate, as this would make it more likely that I would be able to access the memories I was seeking. The lighting was low as we had turned off the overhead spotlights and just used the two small table lamps that we had in the room.
I remember thinking I must be mad as I lay back in the semi darkness on the comfortable couch, which had been prepared for this very purpose. I heard the therapist counting backwards and then I was gone…

I recognised myself as a small baby cradled in my mother's arms. I watched as my father greeted his grandma, a fine-featured silver haired lady who was smiling at us from a rustic doorway.
It was a cold day, so once they had embraced we quickly went inside into a cosy kitchen with a warm fire blazing in the grate.
After the usual pleasantries had been exchanged the attention quickly turned to me.
My dad, Rupert, told his grandma that they had chosen the name Beryl for me and asked if she approved.
For a moment or two my great grandmother was shaken when she heard this name. She looked closely at me and flash of joyous recognition flickered in her wise old eyes. "I cannot begin to tell you how happy I am about the name of this child," she uttered almost incredulously, "I once had a dear friend named Beryl, but that seems a very long time ago."
Sarah then asked, "May I hold her?"
Taking me gently into her own arms as if I were something really precious to her, she walked across the room so that we were as far away as possible from my parents.
Leaning forward so that no one else present could hear, Sarah Susannah Maughan whispered, "We meet again my little one and on this occasion we have no need to defy the laws of time to do so."

"I always hoped we would"

The Secrets of 24 Blackwellgate - Book Two

Sarah Susannah with her special little baby girl...

EPILOGUE

Before I married my name was Beryl Maughan and although this may sound strange, I once had a friend from the past.
We lost touch with each other during the course of living our lives.
Then we met again in the here and now and our story was complete.

My father and I used to speak of Sarah Susannah often.
Rupert once told me that I had been good for her.
He insisted that after that first trip of mine to Burrill to meet her, her whole demeanour changed. She still grieved for her husband of course, but now she had a new light in her eyes and took a great interest in me. She often remarked how much I reminded her of Locryn and of happy adventures in the past.
She also used to say how grateful she was for the long and incredible life she had lived and the wonderful people who had featured in it.

When, in 1946 at the age of ninety-one, she succumbed to her final illness, just as he had done once before when she had been very sick, Rupert refused to leave her.
He kept a vigil by her bed for several days and nights.
He told me she passed away very peacefully, but he still had a bittersweet tear in his eye when he recalled how he was there at her side, holding onto her hand, until the very end.

The Secrets of 24 Blackwellgate - Book Two

I like to think that although my Sarah has slipped gently through the gates of this life, she is surely now at peace, or even (which, knowing her is more likely), continuing her adventures in another...

Footnotes:

The name Maughan has two main geographical sources.
The family name Maughan originated in the Cornish village of Mawgan and was used as a surname by the inhabitants of that place.
There was also a branch of the Maughan family in Ireland.

Maughan's are said to have gypsy blood in their veins. The females of the clan are often gifted with magical powers.

FAMILY ALBUM

For many of us (myself included), photographs are amongst our most treasured possessions. They are moments in time frozen for eternity, for us to revisit whenever we feel the need. They can bring a smile to our face or a tear to our eye, or inspire all the emotions in between. In short they have the power to bridge time and because of that are truly magical...
On the next pages are some family images of our own, which greatly assisted me when I was 'putting flesh onto the bones' of some of the characters in 'Thicker Than Water' so I hope you too can relate them to their counterparts in that story!

1. This image of my paternal great grandmother Sarah Susannah Maughan (seen here with her children Barbara and George), was my inspiration for the character Sarah Maughan (nee Wheeler), as she was in her married life.
   2. Sarah photographed in later life outside her cottage in Burrill, with her son George and young grandson, Rupert.
   3. Young Rupert (my dad), first as a cadet and then in his Black Watch uniform.
   4. Rupert, as a sergeant in The Green Howards training other soldiers to shoot. (He is the second man in from the front of the photograph).
   5. In this photograph I was only a few months old when I was taken to meet my great grandmother. It was said at the time that Sarah whispered something to me that no one else could hear...
   6. My maternal grandmother Annie Fishburn's collection of keys are the subject of this image. Annie (or Nana Fish as we used to call her), never threw a key away but kept them all, as they all had significance to her life. I am now the custodian of these keys.
I do the same with photographs as Nana Fish did with keys. I keep them ALL. To me photographs are the keys to the past.

The Secrets of 24 Blackwellgate - Book Two

This image of my paternal great grandmother Sarah Susannah Maughan (seen here with her children Barbara and George), was my inspiration for the character Sarah Maughan (nee Wheeler), as she was in her married life.

The Secrets of 24 Blackwellgate - Book Two

Sarah photographed in later life outside her cottage in Burrill, with her son George and young grandson, Rupert.

The Secrets of 24 Blackwellgate - Book Two

Young Rupert (my dad) as a young cadet.

Rupert in his Black Watch uniform.

The Secrets of 24 Blackwellgate - Book Two

Rupert, as a sergeant in The Green Howards training other soldiers to shoot. (He is the second man in from the front of the photograph).

The Secrets of 24 Blackwellgate - Book Two

In this photograph I was only a few months old when I was taken to meet my great grandmother. It was said at the time that Sarah whispered something to me that no one else could hear...

The Secrets of 24 Blackwellgate - Book Two

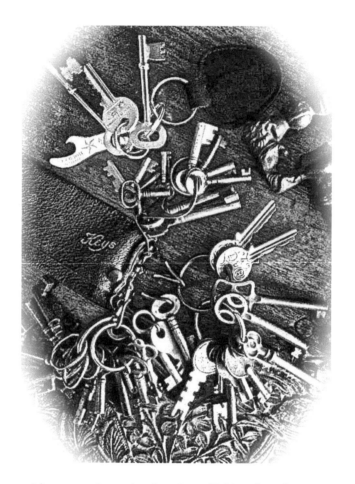

My maternal grandmother Annie Fishburn's collection of keys are the subject of this image. Annie (or Nana Fish as we used to call her), never threw a key away but kept them all, as they all had significance to her life. I am now the custodian of these keys.
I do the same with photographs as Nana Fish did with keys. I keep them ALL. To me photographs are the keys to the past.

THE OBJECTS OF 24 BLACKWELLGATE

Just as photographs can inspire and affect us emotionally, so can certain objects.

This book series is a perfect example of that happening, as it would not have existed if that kind lady who was clearing out the attic of her old farmhouse, in preparation for a move, had not brought two carriers containing some historical clothing and other things into Guru Boutique for us.

I can remember her words now, "I found these things in our attic and rather than take them to a charity shop, I thought I would bring them to you as I knew you would appreciate them.

There are a pair of shoes amongst them, which were made right here in Blackwellgate!"

How right she was.

To me they were fascinating treasures from a time gone by and food for the imagination. Particularly, as she had so rightly assumed, the pair of well-worn hand made ivory kid leather girl's shoes, with the maker's name and location stamped inside. These shoes were the inspiration for three tales featuring an exceptional person called Sarah Wheeler and her family and friends.

Tales which, (you could almost say), wrote themselves.

There now follows half a dozen images of some special objects, which are to be permanently found in our building, or have had some powerful connection to it from time to time…

This is how I envisage Sarah as a young girl. Our friend Courtney, modelling the genuine Victorian maid's outfit which we were so kindly given.

The Secrets of 24 Blackwellgate - Book Two

Spats & Shoes - just some of the aged objects we were kindly given. The spats remind me of my great Uncle George who always wore them when he came to Darlington to visit the Music Hall. The shoes of course were the trigger which started this series off in the first place. You can just see the name of the maker (A Wheeler - Blackwellgate), stamped on the insole.

1 THE MONKEY SKULL

It seems so long ago now since this happened, but I will never forget it or him.
The "him" I refer to is a friend who was the gentlest person that anyone could ever imagine. Some would probably call him a hippy, but he was simply himself.
David was slight in build with longish light brown wavy hair. He usually wore a green hooded camouflage jacket; denim jeans and a granddad shirt. His only adornments were a few raggedy friendship bands around his wrists.
He almost always had a camera and a small canvas bag with him, both of which he carried slung across his body.
He was a man of few possessions.
I knew the bag would contain a notebook, a sketchbook and some pencils, as my friend was a keen botanist and freelance wildlife artist. There might also be some fruit and a container for water in there in case he got hungry or thirsty, whilst out on his daily observations.
Almost every morning on my way down to work I would pass him as he headed into the countryside on the edges of town. He visited several ponds and other sites of interest, where he would keep records of and sketch, newts, frogs, fauna and flowers. This is what he did and he had a good reputation for his knowledge, accuracy and attention to detail. These skills of his secured him satisfying work illustrating several prestigious books and articles for well-known naturalists and their publishers.
We would always stop and chat for a while on these morning encounters and later on in the day, when he had completed his work, he would often call into the place where I work to either buy incense sticks or just to tell us a bit about his day.
All of us in the shop liked this gentle and talented soul very much.
Once a year he made a backpacking trip to a certain place in India for a special festival. Whilst he was there he would go off alone to sketch wildlife and temples and any other interesting things that caught his

eye. He usually stayed over there for a few months, returning here in the spring to resume his work.

Towards the end of 2004 just before he was due to leave for India on his annual trip, he called in to see me bearing a parting gift. I was a little taken aback when I saw that my gift was the skull of a small monkey, but I accepted it with grace and gratitude, as anything which came from David would have special meaning.

He handed it over and then with a little nervous laugh, looked ruefully at me and joked, "I probably shouldn't be giving this away, maybe I'll be cursed or something for doing it." I answered, "I blooming well hope not!"

We both smiled at that and I said I hoped he would have a great time in India and then we said our goodbyes.

Christmas and New Year came and went and then one morning towards the end of January I had the radio on, as usual, whilst making breakfast.

I heard the newsreader say, "a British man from the North East of England has been fatally shot during a festival in a small town in India." Then they named him and I went icy cold and started crying, because it was our friend.

The tragedy was that his killers had shot him in the back, whilst he was peacefully sitting on a bank sketching a temple, in order to rob him. David had very little anyway and if they had asked him to, he would have willingly handed what he did have over and probably wished them well to boot.

I started to think about the last time I saw him and remembered his words about the monkey skull.

I now wondered if indeed the skull was some magical talisman and so at the first opportunity I took it out of the drawer in my office at the shop, where I had put it in for safe keeping. I looked at it carefully and it seemed innocent enough. David did tell me what species of monkey it had come from but I had forgotten. I decided that in view of what had happened it was best to take no chances, so I put it in a very safe place on my desk where it couldn't get knocked off or mislaid. I also

The Secrets of 24 Blackwellgate - Book Two

told myself that due to it being a room, which only members of staff at the shop had access to, it would be the safest place to keep it. That was 2005 and the monkey skull has been in its place on my desk ever since. I look at it often and think of my friend and wonder… I will never part with it of course, as who knows what might happen if I did.

I include this true story as a tribute to an exceptional human being and friend.

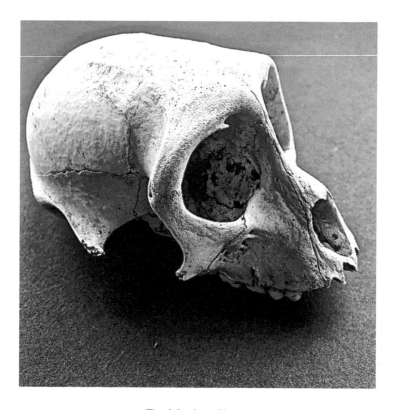

The Monkey Skull...

2 DAISY DUNN'S TINY TEAPOT

This is an item in my possession, which is a sort of family heirloom. Nothing expensive you understand, in fact quite the opposite, a humble little white teapot.
This tiny teapot has a sad story attached to it.
Way back in the late nineteen twenties its original owner, a girl called Daisy, lived down the street from my grandparent's house. Nana and granddad had two children. Their son was Humphrey and their daughter was Irene. Irene was a lovely young girl who would eventually become my mother.
I wasn't born then of course, as at that point my mam wasn't even courting.
The house where Daisy lived didn't have many facilities, so she used to call round to have a wash sometimes when we had heated enough water to share with her. Irene and Daisy became firm friends. Daisy who was a little older than Irene was already married to a handsome young husband, but he was very strict with her. She had already revealed to her friend that she feared his disapproval.
One day when she called for her bathing session, she brought her friend a gift. It was a tiny white teapot, no more than four inches high, with a design running around it in vertical stripes and a hinged pewter lid. Irene loved it and Daisy assured her that although it wasn't marked as such, it was, 'Wedgwood' – whether it was or not doesn't really matter. It was treasured anyway.
When she had finished bathing Daisy had to dash away, as she knew how angry her husband would be if she was late home to make his evening meal. She was running down the street when she slipped and fell. That fall proved fatal as according to Irene, who related the story to me many years later, "she twisted something inside."
From that day on the little teapot had pride of place on the mantelpiece in every house where my mother lived, in memory of sweet Daisy.

The Secrets of 24 Blackwellgate - Book Two

Now all these years later my mam has passed away too and it is now mine to take care of. I treasure it just as much as she always did. I always think of both Irene and of Daisy when I look at it.

I have no children of my own to pass this special object down to so that is why I am telling you.

Daisy Dunne's tiny teapot.

3 BAND OF GOLD

Only once in my life have I ever been to a Spiritualists Church, but the time I did go I had felt compelled to attend. My friend Kelly (who had kindly agreed to go with me) and I slipped in late and sat right at the very back trying to be inconspicuous. Not far into the experience, one of the mediums on the stage looked in our direction, pointed and said, "the dark haired lady at the back." Kelly nudged me saying, "I think he means you." I stood up and the medium told me, "I have your parents here. Your mother says you should always wear the ring, and your father just said, 'that's my girl,' I hope these things mean something to you?" Then he had moved on to someone else. I was stunned. The fact that my dad had said what he said convinced me there was something in this, as that is what he always said about me. A shiver ran down my spine and I felt a little dizzy. As for the mention of a ring by my mam, I was a bit puzzled. Then I remembered that I had amongst my souvenirs of her, a thin gold wedding band that had grown too loose for her fingers, which she had given to me for safekeeping. I went home in a daze and the first thing I did was look for the ring. It would only fit my little finger, but I immediately put it on and have worn it ever since.

Footnote: Similarly my mam (Irene) had only ever been to a Spiritualists church once in her lifetime too. On that occasion she too went along with a friend.

Irene had been married to my father, Rupert since she was 18 and was now 26 so they had given up any hope of having children. Anyway, one of the mediums singled her out just as I had been singled out the one time I had gone. She came and stood in front of my mother and made a rocking movement with her arms as if she was soothing a baby, and said, "Soon after the corn has been sown and reaped you will be doing this." My mam laughed and whispered to her friend, "I don't think so!" The same year that prediction which had been made by the Medium almost miraculously came true, as Irene became pregnant.

In December that year I was born.

I am her only child.

Band of Gold.

4 PADFOOT AND THE TEN BOB NOTE

I've not had many supernatural experiences in my life, but when I was about twelve I may have encountered a Hell Hound.
This is what happened.
My dad was the caretaker of Springfield School in Salter's Lane South and my mam was the head cleaner there.
We lived in a bungalow called Rockwell, which was attached to the school grounds. There was a big playing field at the back of our house belonging to the school and the actual Rock Well was supposed to have been down in the bottom corner of this field at one time before it was covered over.
One day I was at the back of our house playing in the field when suddenly, out of no-where it seemed, a huge snarling creature that looked like a cross between a lion and a large dog appeared…
I should have been scared as it was really large and unlike any animal I had ever seen before, but instead I put my hand out to calm it and went closer. I started talking to it saying, "Stay there and I'll go and get you something to eat!" I turned to go to the house for some food and then glanced back to make sure the beast was all right, but now there was nothing there. It had vanished and was nowhere to be seen in the big field. It would have been impossible for it to have simply run away as I would have seen it in the distance…

Just then my aunty arrived from Stockton and this was unusual, as she had not visited us at this house before. She was very, very, nice to everyone and even gave me a ten-shilling note, which was quite a lot of money in those days. She stayed for tea and then left to get the bus back home…
Two days later we heard she had taken her own life, so it seems obvious that the poor lady came to see us to say her goodbyes. Later on in my life I read about a legendary hellhound, which had appeared throughout history, in our area, called 'Padfoot' or 'the Barquest of Throstle Nest' and It was said that this apparition

The Secrets of 24 Blackwellgate - Book Two

(amongst other things) was a harbinger of death. It was described as a large dog-like creature, which roamed the area from a place called Throstle Nest (off Haughton Road) to Salter's Lane and an area known as Springfield.
To this day I wonder if the creature I met was this same beast.
P.S. I keep one of the old ten bob notes in my purse to this day in memory of my Aunty Annie and it comes with me to number 24 Blackwellgate every day that I am at work.
It is not the same one of course, as I spent that back when I was a youngster back in the 1950's - but it does have meaning for me.

Ten bob note obscuring a mysterious hound.

Footnotes:

A friend of ours called Chuck Rutland added a little more to this legend. He informed me that as well as being a harbinger of death these hounds (and apparently there are legends concerning sightings of hell hounds in other parts of the country too), have also been known to save lives by appearing to warn people of impending disaster.
Legend tells us that on a particular dark and stormy night one of these beasts barred a road above Whitby. It would not let anyone pass. This was in the days of the stagecoach. So when a coach came along and the driver saw the terrifying dog, he took his passengers back into the town. When the coach set off again the next day in daylight they discovered that a bridge they had intended to cross was broken and they would no doubt all have been killed if they had tried to cross it on the previous night.

Another friend, Sylvia Clement tells me the name 'barquest' comes from the Danish and means 'carriage for the dead!'

5 JOAN OF WAD AND JACK 'O' THE LANTERN

I have a souvenir from the past that Vyvyan, 'the Cornish witch' in the story 'THICKER THAN WATER would have been familiar with. It is a little brown leather purse containing some small figurines depicting two mythical characters from Cornish folklore, known as Joan of Wad and Jack 'o' the Lantern.
I inherited these items from my grandmother.
She carried them with her all the time, as she believed they would protect her and bring her good luck. She didn't do too badly in life either, as in spite of smoking woodbines from the age of eleven years old, she managed to live to the ripe old age of ninety seven - and would have gone on for much longer, I am certain, had it not been for an unfortunate fall. I only mention this to illustrate that she had been a lucky lady and definitely not to promote smoking.

Here's a bit of information about Joan of Wad:
She is revered for being the Queen of the Pixies (or as they are sometimes known, Piskeys). Her last name Wad is a Cornish term for a torch made from a bundle of straw.
She has a male equivalent, Jack 'o' the Lantern who is said to be the King of the Pixies. So, they both represent light in the darkness and people thought that carrying little effigies of these two mythical figures with them all the time, would keep them safe.

There is even a little rhyme that my grandmother used to recite, and it goes as follows…
'Jack-the-lantern, Joan-the-wad,
That tickled the maid and made her mad,
Light me home, the weather's bad.'
Joan the Wad was also thought to use her Wad (Torch) to light the way to safety and good luck, and a second rhyme goes as follows,
'Good fortune will nod, if you carry upon you Joan the Wad.'

The Secrets of 24 Blackwellgate - Book Two

Joan of Wad & Jack'O'Lantern. These lucky charms which depict characters from Cornish Folklore were very popular in times gone by.

6 SARAH SUSANNAH'S LAMP

Whenever I see oil lamps I marvel at the fact that they illuminated our homes on the long dark nights, long before the luxury we experience today of having electricity at the touch of a switch. I am overjoyed to say that many years ago a very special example of one of these lamps, which has been handed down through the generations in my family, came into my possession.
It is shown in the accompanying photograph and it once lit the kitchen of a cottage my ancestors inhabited in the North Yorkshire countryside. This is very possibly the only item that remains in our family, which was personally owned by my great grandmother, a beautiful, dignified person who was loved and respected by all who knew her, the wonderful Sarah Susannah Maughan. My own mother always described her to me as being, "a real Victorian lady with a lovely complexion," who spoke gently, and was always exquisitely dressed in long gowns with high collars, embellished by a broach. In her later life these gowns were always black, in memory of her late husband. I was lucky enough to physically encounter Sarah Susannah, shortly before she became ill and subsequently passed away.

I don't know how an object so fragile as her lamp, complete with the original glass, has managed to survive throughout so many years - but it has and now sits proudly atop its ornate brass base as a prized object amongst my souvenirs.
It not only links me to her and to the past, but also acts as a symbol of continuity, lighting the way into the future...

The Secrets of 24 Blackwellgate - Book Two

Sarah Susannah's lamp. It's now one of my most treasured possessions, as it links me to my own great grandmother and to the past.

TRICK OR TREAT?

On Halloween, 2018 - the very day this volume was put out for pre-sale and just before it finally went to print, something quite extraordinary happened in 24, Blackwellgate.
Although this occurrence took place when, as far as I was concerned, this book was done, I feel it must be included.
So here it is…
It was a suitably atmospheric Halloween in Darlington with lots happening inside and outside our shop. There was spooky street theatre going on in town, shop windows and public houses were decorated to celebrate the festival, people in fancy dress were to be seen around town and there was a lantern parade planned for later on.
I even joined in by dressing up at work in a skeleton dress, as a nod to this special day. The guys I work with in Guru thought I was mad for doing it, so I said I'd only wear the dress until noon and then change back into my usual work outfit again.
All morning we'd had a succession of weird and wonderful people popping in to see us, so it was no surprise and in fact, a real treat, when two spooky looking undertakers walked in. They were actually a street theatre act known as Trick and Treat (aka Mark and Maggie). We enjoyed their visit enormously. Katie Greenwood, who works for Darlington Council, was with them and she even took a photo of Trick and Treat and I, and sent it to my phone. I thought this was definitely the high spot of our day, but there was more to come…
They had just left and I was showing a girl (who looked a lot like Mother of Dragons from Game Of Thrones) some crystals, when a striking looking dark haired lady came into the shop. She had a real presence and I noticed her straight away. She looked me over (approvingly I thought), smiled and made a beeline for where I was standing and started a conversation with 'Mother of Dragons' and myself. I couldn't quite place her accent but it certainly wasn't one from around here.

I'm not quite sure how the topic came up, but the lady suddenly looked directly at me and said, "It's not good to have a skull in your house you know!"

I pointed at our Gothic cabinet and asked her, "Do you mean these resin skull ornaments we sell?" She replied, "No, I mean a real skull…"

I said, "Oh, dear, I do have a real skull, but it's not in my house, it's here in the shop," and proceeded to tell her about the monkey skull that I have on my desk in the office upstairs, adding, "It was a gift from a dear friend and I will never part with it."

(You, the reader will know the story of the skull already as I wrote about it earlier in this book).

Her voice was almost hypnotic as she continued, "Mmmm, there is no need to part with it, but you must move it immediately from where it is now. It needs to be cleansed of any malevolence and kept in the lowest part of the building."

In spite of my natural scepticism, as I do know there are many charlatans out there, I was taking this very seriously. There was something very compelling about this lady. After all, how had she known I owned a skull in the first place?

She nodded understandingly and then proceeded to tell me how I could remove any negative aspects associated with the little skull. She told me to carry it into the basement as soon as possible and perform a ritual over it, involving cinnamon, incense and flame. She told me exactly what to do and even told me when to hold the cinnamon in my left hand and when to sprinkle it on the skull with my right. Finally she added, "Halloween is the very best time for you to do this essential task. I was meant to come here today."

She then wished me luck and turned to leave… "Thank you, but I don't even know your name," I called after her.

She turned back and fixed me with a stare from her incredible grey/green eyes and said, "It's Vyvyan."

The Secrets of 24 Blackwellgate - Book Two

Postscript: I didn't dare ask to take a photo of the mysterious lady, but I have included the one of Mark and Maggie (aka Trick and Treat) and myself which Katie took, to illustrate the strangeness of the day when all this happened.

Needless to say my monkey skull, now suitably cleansed, resides safely locked inside a glass cabinet in our basement.